A Treasury of Children's CLASSICS

Commissioning Editor   Christine Deverell
Additional Illustrations   Richard Deverell
Design   Ian Jones

©2000 Robert Frederick Limited
4-5 North Parade
Bath, U.K.
BA1 1LF

Printed in China

A Treasury of
Children's
CLASSICS

THREE FAIRY TALES
Adapted by
CHRISTINE DEVERELL

· C O N T E N T S ·

Sleeping Beauty

ILLUSTRATED BY JAN NESBITT

A long time ago there lived a King and Queen who were very sad, because they had no children. One day, as the Queen sat by a pond in the castle gardens thinking of her wishes, a frog hopped on to a lily pad in front of her and said, "Your wish will be granted. Before a year has passed, you shall have a daughter."

Everything happened as the frog had said. A little girl was born, and the King was so happy that he ordered a great celebration feast to be held. All their friends and relatives, and Kings and Queens from other kingdoms were invited, together with twelve fairies who would bring special gifts to the Princess.

Now it happened that there were thirteen such fairies living in this domain, and everyone knows that thirteen is an unlucky number. So one of these was not invited to the feast, and she was not a happy fairy. The day for the feast arrived and all the guests were gathered in the Great Hall of the King's castle. Every guest brought a gift, and the twelve fairies lined up to bestow their special gifts on the baby.

"I give her virtue," said one. "I give her beauty," said another. Yet another gave her riches, another health and so on, until she had all the gifts that any mother or father could wish their child to own. Eleven fairies gave their gifts, and as the twelfth stepped forward, the door flew open, and in marched the thirteenth who was determined to have her revenge.

"On her fifteenth birthday the Princess shall prick her finger on a needle and die!" she exclaimed loudly, and turned her back on the whole company and left. Then the twelfth fairy, who had not yet given her gift, stepped forward. She said that she could not undo the wicked fairy's curse, but she could soften it.

"The King's daughter will not die, but will sleep for a hundred years." But the King and Queen hoped to save their daughter from this fate, and ordered that all the needles in the Kingdom should be destroyed.

The Princess grew to be beautiful, wise, friendly and well behaved. Everyone who knew her, loved her.

Now it happened that on the morning of the day of her fifteenth birthday, the King and Queen were not at home, so the Princess was alone in the castle.

She wandered around from room to room, along the corridors and up and down the splendid staircases until she came upon an old tower. She climbed the narrow, winding stairs until she reached a door, in the lock of which was a rusty key. The Princess turned the key, the door sprang open, and there in the room she saw an old woman with a spinning wheel. "Good morning, my good lady," said the Princess, "what are you doing here?" "I am spinning," she replied, "here, you can try it."

No sooner had she taken hold of the spindle, the Princess pricked her finger and fell back onto a bed in a deep sleep. Everyone in the castle fell asleep; The King and Queen who had just returned home, their courtiers and servants. The horses in the stable, the doves on the roof, the flies on the walls, and even the fire in the hearth all appeared to die in the same moment.

A thick bramble hedge quickly grew around the castle until not even the flag on the high tower could be seen. The story was told throughout many lands of the beautiful Princess asleep in a lost castle where every living creature lay motionless.

Many princes came and tried to cut their way through the thorns to reach her, but they were unsuccessful. After many years had passed, another King's son came by and heard the story of the sleeping Princess. He was not to be daunted by the failure of those who had gone before him.

It happened that one hundred years had very nearly passed since the great sleep had fallen on the castle. As this young Prince approached the thick, bramble hedge, the thorns turned into fine flowers and parted to let him through.

In the courtyard he saw the horses and dogs lying fast asleep. He stepped over the bodies of the courtiers in the Great Hall and saw the King and Queen asleep on their thrones.

The Prince looked in all the rooms in the castle, and at last he came to the tower and opened the door of the little chamber where the Princess slept. She looked so beautiful that the Prince

could not help but gaze upon her, and he bent down and kissed her. Just as he did so, she opened her eyes and smiled at him.

Then the King and Queen awoke, and the whole court, the servants, the horses, the dogs and the flies on the wall. The fire in the hearth began to burn brightly. The whole castle was once more alive with the sound of happy voices as if nothing had happened, for the hundred years sleep had made no difference to anyone.

Very soon, the wedding of The Prince and his Sleeping Beauty was celebrated with great splendour, and they lived together happy and contented to the end of their lives.

The Wolf & the Seven Little Goats

I L L U S T R A T E D   B Y   K A T E   D A V I E S

Once upon a time there lived a Nanny Goat who had seven young kids. She loved them as any mother loves her children. One day, she wanted to go into the forest, so she called the little goats together and said, "Dear children, I am going away into the wood; be on your guard against the wolf. If he comes here, he will eat you all up.

He may try to fool you into thinking he is someone else, but you will know him by his gruff voice and his black feet." "Don't worry, mother," the little goats replied, "we'll remember." So she went on her way, quite happily. Not long after the mother goat had gone, there was a knock at the door and a voice called out, "Open the door, children; your mother is here and has brought something for each of you."

23

But the little goats knew from the gruff voice that it was the wolf, so they said, "No, you cannot come in, you are not our mother. She has a kind and gentle voice, but yours is gruff; you are a wolf." So the wolf went home and found a piece of chalk, which he ate. This made his voice more gentle, so he returned to the goats' house, knocked at the door and called out, "Open, my dear children; your mother has come home and brought you each something." But the wolf had placed his paws on the window sill.

When the little goats saw them they said, "No, no, we will not open the door to you. Our mother has white paws, and yours are black. You are a wolf."

So the wolf went to a baker and said, "I have hurt my foot, put some dough on it." When the baker had done this, the wolf ran to the miller saying, "Put some white flour on my feet." But the miller, thinking the wolf was planning to fool someone, refused. But then the wolf said to him, "If you do not do what I ask, I will eat you." The miller was afraid, and powdered the wolf's feet with flour. Now, the wicked wolf went for a third time to the goats' house and knocked on the door. "Open up to me dear children; your mother is come, and I have brought you something nice from the forest."

He put his paws up on the window sill, and when the little goats saw that they were white, they thought it was safe, and they undid the door. Then who should come in but the wolf! They were so frightened, they ran and hid themselves. One ran under the table, the second crawled under the bed, the third hid in the cupboard, the fourth behind the kitchen door, the fifth in the oven, the sixth in the wash tub and the seventh in the big grandfather clock.

The wolf found them out, and quickly swallowed them up, one after the other; the only little goat he did not discover was in the grandfather clock.

The wolf could hardly move, but dragged himself into the forest, where he lay down to sleep. Soon the little goats' mother came home. What a terrible sight greeted her. The door was wide open; the table, stools and benches were overturned, the wash tub was broken in pieces, and the sheets were pulled off the bed. She

27

could not find her children anywhere.

She called them all by name, but they did not appear, until she came to the name of the youngest: "Here I am, mother, in the grandfather clock." When the little one came out, she told her mother what the wolf had done, and they hugged each

other and cried. They went out for a walk in the forest, and they came to a glade where they found the wolf sleeping. The mother goat walked right round the wolf as he lay there snoring, and she thought she saw something moving inside him.

"Oh my goodness!" she whispered to herself, "could it be that my poor children are still alive?"

They ran home to fetch a pair of scissors, needle and thread. Then the mother cut open the wicked wolf's hairy coat and out popped a little head. One little goat jumped out, followed by another, then another, until all six were set free. Not one of them was hurt, because the greedy monster had swallowed them all whole!

They danced and sang and hugged each other, and their mother said, "Quickly, go and fetch as many stones as you can find, so we can fill up the wolf's stomach before he wakes up." They gathered a pile of huge stones, and put them into his stomach. Their mother sewed up the slit with the needle and thread, and all the while, the greedy wolf did not stir.

When at last he woke up, he was very thirsty and went to a stream to have a drink. But as he rolled along from side to side, the stones tumbled about inside his body and he cried out:

> *"What rattles, what rattles*
>
> > *Against my poor bones?*
>
> *Not little goats, I think,*
>
> > *But only big stones!"*

When the wolf reached the edge of the stream he bent down to take a drink, and the heavy stones made him lose his balance, so that he fell, and sank beneath the water. All the while the little goats and their mother were watching from behind the trees. When they saw the big splash, they came running up, singing, "The wolf is dead! the wolf is dead!" and they danced for joy around their mother by the side of the stream.

The Frog Prince

ILLUSTRATED BY IVANA SVABIC CANNON

34

Long ago there lived a king with several beautiful daughters. But the youngest was so beautiful that even the Sun himself was enchanted when she came out to play in the sunshine. She would often go out into the garden by herself, and one afternoon she was dancing around on the grass, throwing a golden ball up into the air and catching it again.

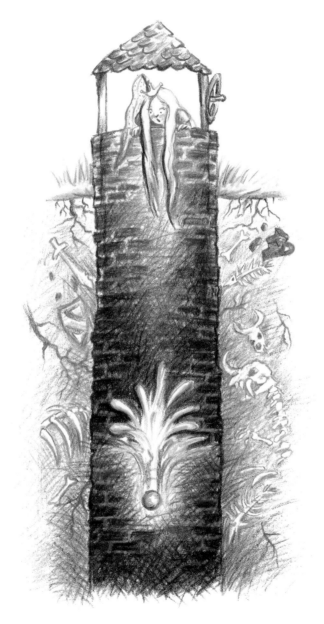

The ball glinted in the sunshine and the Princess missed catching it when for a moment the bright light blinded her eyes.

She laughed as she ran down the slope chasing after it. Then she threw the golden ball high into the air and watched in horror as it fell into a well so deep that it seemed to take forever before she heard a feint plop as it hit the water at the bottom.

The Princess sat down beside the well and wept. She cried louder and louder until she heard a voice call out, "Why are you crying O King's daughter? Your tears would melt even a stone to pity." She looked around to the spot where the voice was coming from and saw a Frog's ugly face staring at her.

"Was it you that spoke? I am weeping for my golden ball which has fallen into this well and I don't know how I will ever get it back." "Never mind," said the Frog, "I can get it back for you. But what will you give me if I do?" "What would you like, dear Frog? You can have my jewels, my pearls or my golden crown." "I have no use for these things," replied the Frog, "but if you will love me, and let me play with you, sit at your table, eat from your plate, drink from your cup, and sleep in your bed, then I will climb into the well and retrieve your golden ball."

"Oh, I will promise you all these things, if only I can have
my ball," she cried, thinking that she would never have to keep
a promise she made to a Frog. But the Frog dropped into the
well, picked up the golden ball in his mouth and climbed all the
way out. The Princess thanked him, took the ball and ran off, as
fast as she could, back to the palace. "Stop! Stop! Wait for me!
I cannot keep up with you," croaked the Frog in his loudest
voice, but she did not even hear him.

The Princess soon forgot the Frog and the promise she had made, and the frog hopped back into the lake near the well. One day, the King's daughter was sitting at table with her father and his courtiers when she heard a knock at the door. She went to open it and there before her stood the Frog. The Princess turned very pale and quickly shut the door. As she sat down to eat again her father asked her if there was a giant at the door to frighten

her so. "No father, it is not a giant, but an ugly Frog." "And what does the Frog want?" said the King. The Princess told her father the story of how she lost her golden ball in the well and the promise she made to the Frog. Then the King said, "A promise made must be kept.

Go and let him in." So reluctantly she went and opened the door and the Frog followed her back to her place. "Pick me up," he said, and the King ordered her to obey. She placed the Frog on her chair, and immediately he sprang up onto the table and demanded, "Move your plate close to me and we will eat together."

Everyone at the table could see she was very unwilling, but she did what she had promised. The Frog relished every mouthful but the King's daughter felt sick and could not eat any more of her food. When she got down from the table she lifted the Frog

onto the floor and he followed her
out into the garden to play. The
little Frog went everywhere with
her and when she thought she could
escape from him, she ran as fast as
she could back to the palace.
Remembering her promise that
she would let the Frog sleep in
her bed, she ran straight upstairs
to her bedroom and
bolted the door. Just as
the Princess got into
bed, she heard a feint
knocking sound.

"Who's there?" she called, her voice trembling. "Please let me in; you promised I could sleep in your bed, and your father said a promise made must be kept." The Princess opened the door and the Frog hopped across the room and clambered up onto the bed. The frightened girl curled up as far away from the Frog as she could, but was unable to sleep all night.

The next day, the little Frog refused to leave the Princess's side. He played with her, sat on her lap when she rode with her father in his carriage and ate from her plate at meal times. The poor girl was growing tired of this ugly little creature and feared she might never be rid of him. "Will you never go away and leave me alone, you ugly little Frog?" she asked him tearfully. "First, you must kiss me, and then if

you really want me to leave you sweet Princess, I will go." Kiss a Frog? The poor girl thought she would rather die. But so desperate was she to be free of him that she took a deep breath, closed her eyes, and offered him her lips to kiss.

When she opened her eyes she found that the Frog had indeed disappeared, and in his place stood a tall, handsome young Prince.

He told her how a wicked witch had transformed him and that only she could set him free from the spell. She fell in love with him instantly and they ran back to the palace to find her father. He gave his consent to their marriage and the Prince and Princess lived very happily in his kingdom for many years.